About this book:

Amazing Mrs Oberon is a grandmother in a million. Not only is she expert at trailbiking, fearless at shooting rapids, a skilful pilot, and a whizz on a skateboard, but when it comes to baking, her cock-a-hoop-honey-cake beats all others. And when her teething grandson needs soothing, Mrs Oberon combines her talents in a mission of mercy – with spectacular results.

'The queen of children's fiction.' – *Independent on Sunday*

Chosen for Children's Books of the Year 1994

HAMBONE HILLS

Riff-Raff Rapids

Mrs Oberon's House

SWAGWALLOW SWAMP

For Alice, with grandmotherly love – MM

For Ian, with love – MC

A Busy Day for a Good Grandmother

MARGARET MAHY

Illustrated by Margaret Chamberlain

PUFFIN BOOKS

Mrs Oberon was quietly cleaning her trailbike at her home in the rugged Hambone hills. Sitting on the veranda rail, her seven cats waited patiently to be fed.

"Milk in a minute!" said Mrs Oberon. But at that moment the phone rang. It was her son, Scrimshaw. He was in a terrible state.

"Oh, Mother, Mother! Wanda's gone to work, and it's my turn to look after little Sweeney. He's cutting his top teeth, and he's weeping and wailing and carrying on something awful. What he needs is a soothing slice of your cock-a-hoop-honey-cake."

"Well, give him a slice, then, Scrimshaw," suggested Mrs Oberon.

"Oh, Mother, we've eaten the cock-a-hoop-honey-cake you sent last week, and I don't know how to make another," wailed Scrimshaw.

"By a lucky chance I have a freshly baked cock-a-hoop-honey-cake in my cake tin," said Mrs Oberon. "I'll bring it over at once."

"Wonderful!" cried Scrimshaw, suddenly sounding much more cheerful. "I'll serenade Sweeney on my electric guitar until you arrive."

Mrs Oberon put a huge tin full of cock-a-hoop-honey-cake into her backpack. She also packed a pot of blue borage honey, her skateboard, fifty butcher-bean rissoles (made with home-grown butcher beans), and a batch of healthy – but rather heavy – carrot muffins she had baked before breakfast. The backpack bulged as Mrs Oberon swung it over her strong shoulders. On with her motorbike helmet! A quick vault over the veranda railings, and Mrs Oberon landed lightly on her trailbike, revved up, and was off and away.

There had been one or two small avalanches overnight, but the weight of the carrot muffins stopped the trailbike from bouncing about too much. Mrs Oberon reached the river just where the dangerous Riff-Raff rapids began.

Leaping off her trailbike, she jumped straight over the bank and on to her red racing-raft, tied up below. Rafting in and out of the ragged rocks of the Riff-Raff rapids, she patted her backpack to make sure the cock-a-hoop-honey-cake was safe and sound.

Mrs Oberon swept down the squiggly, wriggly, roundabout river, skilfully pushing herself off shoals and shallows, and cunningly avoiding cross-currents and whirlpools.

At last she shot triumphantly out of the Riff-Raff rapids into the Swagwallow swamp. The red raft was going so fast, it skipped halfway across the swamp before slowing down. Alligators immediately began to close in on Mrs Oberon, smiling and snapping their jaws.

However, she was ready for them. Reaching into her backpack she lightly tossed handfuls of butcher-bean rissoles into the water.

A hideous hurly-burly began. Swagwallow swamp hissed and seethed as alligators fought desperately for the tasty morsels, beating the water with their powerful tails. They all loved the taste of butcher beans. But butcher-bean rissoles are remarkably sticky.

The alligators spent the next twenty minutes trying to free their fangs from the butcher beans while Mrs Oberon poled gracefully in between them, whistling softly to herself.

While this was going on, Scrimshaw was playing the electric guitar, and singing to his poor, teething baby.

"Hush-a-by, baby, with teeth coming through,
Soon you'll have toothypegs, shining and new.
No snarling, my darling, no hullabaloo!
A cock-a-hoop-honey-cake's heading for you!"

Meanwhile, Mrs Oberon had landed her red raft beside Swagwallow airport. Her faithful Piper Cherokee aircraft was waiting at the end of the runway. Mrs Oberon checked the fuel – and the muffin-ejector (an instrument of her own invention). Everything was working well. She took off to the north, flying up and over the Chopper mountain range where pointed, pearly peaks seemed to nibble at the blue edge of the sky.

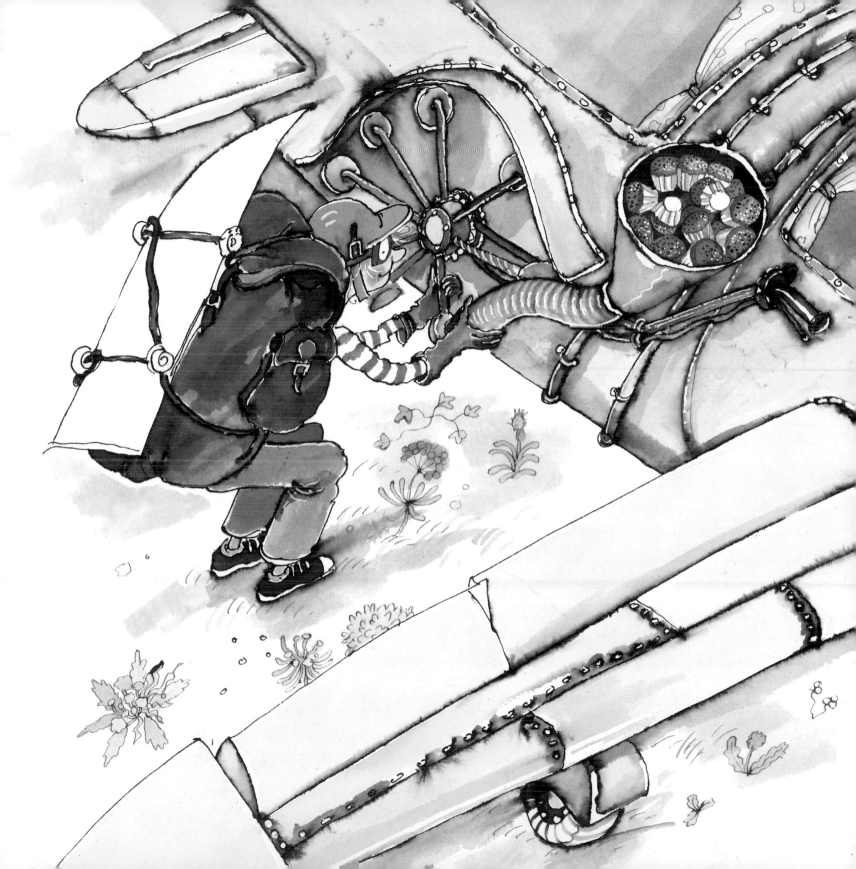

Suddenly, out from a cleft in the mountains soared a sinister swarm of birds.

"Oh dear! Ice vultures!" muttered Mrs Oberon. "I was afraid this might happen."

Exceptionally large ice vultures were settling on the wings of the Piper Cherokee, staring hungrily at Mrs Oberon.

But she was already filling the muffin-ejector tube with carrot muffins. BOOM! Muffins flew high into the clear mountain air. Off went the vultures, greedily snapping up muffins. And as the muffins were rather heavy (however healthy), the vultures immediately lost altitude. They sank slowly out of sight, flapping their wings madly, while Mrs Oberon waved to them from her Piper Cherokee aircraft and headed for the city airport.

Scrimshaw was desperate. Standing on his head, he played the electric guitar upside down, balancing a bowl of fruit salad on one foot to distract his poor baby. As he did this, he sang to Sweeney:

"You've got those teething blues!
Yeah, baby, you've got those teething blues!
The day's going by and there's no good news.
Oh, *wah, wah, waaaaah!*"

But Sweeney howled a *wah, wah, waaaaah* of his own which was even louder than Scrimshaw's.

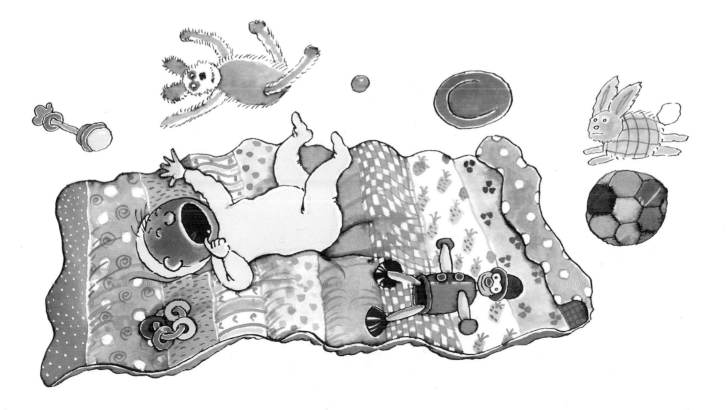

Suddenly, the door burst open. In sailed Mrs Oberon on her skateboard, still wearing her motorbike helmet and her backpack.

Whisking the cake tin from her backpack, she opened it at once.
There, inside, was a great, big, wholesome, healthy, sweet and soothing
cock-a-hoop-honey-cake. How delicious it smelt! Scrimshaw stopped
playing his electric guitar, and Sweeney stopped howling.

Mrs Oberon gave her grandson a huge slice of cake. His sore gums were soothed. His sadness was sweetened. He sighed with happiness, and sank into a soft, smiling sleep. Scrimshaw sighed with happiness, too.

"I'm worn out," he said and, collapsing into a chair, he turned on the television.

"Now, Scrimshaw," his mother cried, "turn off that television and come into the kitchen with me. I am going to show you how to bake cock-a-hoop-honey-cake yourself."

"But I don't have any blue borage honey in the house," cried Scrimshaw quickly. He knew that if he were taught to make cock-a-hoop-honey-cake, he might have to bake his own for ever after . . .

"Never fear, my darling. I brought an extra pot of borage honey with me," said Mrs Oberon with a big smile.

"You think of everything, Mum," cried Scrimshaw, getting out the eggbeater.

So, Mrs Oberon taught him how to bake his own cock-a-hoop-honey-cake, and when the cake was finished she said, "Very good. But now I must go home. Friends are depending on me."

So she went all the way home by skateboard, plane, raft and trailbike.
Vultures and alligators pretended not to see her going by.

And as she vaulted off the trailbike, her cats ran eagerly to meet her.
"It's been a long day," said Mrs Oberon, pouring milk into seven saucers.

Then, at last, she climbed into bed. And in next to no time she was dreaming happily of cock-a-hoop-honey-cake, while the seven cats settled down on her patchwork quilt, purring loudly.

Other Picture Books by Margaret Mahy

THE GREAT WHITE MAN-EATING SHARK   *(with Jonathan Allen)*
A LION IN THE MEADOW   *(with Jenny Williams)*
THE MAN WHOSE MOTHER WAS A PIRATE   *(with Margaret Chamberlain)*
A SUMMERY SATURDAY MORNING   *(with Selina Young)*
THE THREE-LEGGED CAT *(with Jonathan Allen)*
THE WITCH IN THE CHERRY TREE   *(with Jenny Williams)*

PUFFIN BOOKS

Published by the Penguin Group
Penguin Books Ltd, 80 Strand, London WC2R 0RL, England
Penguin Group (USA), Inc., 375 Hudson Street, New York, New York 10014, USA
Penguin Books Australia Ltd, 250 Camberwell Road, Camberwell, Victoria 3124, Australia
Penguin Books Canada Ltd, 10 Alcorn Avenue, Toronto, Ontario, Canada M4V 3B2
Penguin Books (NZ) Ltd, Cnr Rosedale and Airborne Roads, Albany, Auckland, New Zealand
Penguin Books (South Africa) (Pty) Ltd, 24 Sturdee Avenue, Rosebank 2196, South Africa

Penguin Books Ltd, Registered Offices: 80 Strand, London WC2R 0RL, England

www.penguin.com

First published by Hamish Hamilton Ltd 1993
Published in Picture Puffins 1995
20 19 18 17 16 15 14 13 12 11

Text copyright © Margaret Mahy, 1993
Illustrations copyright © Margaret Chamberlain, 1993
All rights reserved

The moral right of the author and illustrator has been asserted

Made and printed in Italy by Printer Trento Srl

A Vanessa Hamilton Book
Designed by Mark Foster

British Library Cataloguing in Publication Data
A CIP catalogue record for this book is available from the British Library

0–140–50227–0